Trouble in Mind

John Harvey

CRIME EXPRESS

Trouble in Mind

by *John Harvey*

Published by Crime Express in 2007
Reprinted in 2008
Crime Express is an imprint of
Five Leaves Publications,
PO Box 8787, Nottingham NG1 9AW

ISBN: 978-1-905512-25-6

Cover design: Richard Hollis
Author photograph: Philip Matsas
Typesetting and design:
Four Sheets Design and Print
Printed in Great Britain

Kiley smoothed the page across his desk and read it again: a survey conducted by Littlewoods Pools had concluded that of all 92 Premiership and Football League soccer teams, the one most likely to cause its supporters severe stress was Notts County. Notts County! Sitting snug, the last time Kiley had looked, near the midpoint of the League Two table and in immediate danger neither of relegation nor the nail-biting possibilities of promotion via the play-offs. Whereas Charlton Athletic, in whose colours Kiley had turned out towards the end of his short and less than illustrious career, were just one place from the bottom of the Premiership, with only four wins out of a possible twenty-two. Not only that, despite having sacked two successive managers before Christmas, this Saturday just passed they had been bundled out of the FA Cup by Nottingham Forest, who had comprehensively stuffed them at the City ground, two-nil.

Stress? Stress didn't even begin to come close.

Kiley looked at the clock.

12.09.

Too late for morning coffee, too early for lunch. From his office window he could see the traffic edging in both directions, a pair of red 134 buses nuzzling up to one another as they prepared to run the gauntlet of Kentish Town Road on their way west towards the city centre, the slow progress of a council recycling lorry holding up those drivers who were heading — God help them — for the Archway roundabout and thence all points north.

His in-tray held a bill from the local processing lab, a begging letter from the Royal National Lifeboat Institution, and a polite reminder from HM Revenue & Customs that the final deadline for filing his tax return was the 31st January — for more details about charges and penalties, see the enclosed leaflet SA352.

His pending file, had he possessed such a thing, would have held details of a course in advanced DNA analysis he'd half-considered after a severe overdose of *CSI*; a letter, handwritten, from a Muswell Hill housewife — a rare, but not extinct breed — wanting to know what Kiley would charge to find out if her husband was slipping around with his office junior — as if — and a second letter, crisply typed on headed note paper, offering employment in a prestigious security firm run by two former colleagues from the Met. Attractive in its way, but Kiley couldn't see himself happily touching his peaked cap to every four-by-four driver checking out of a private estate in Totteridge and Whetstone on the way to collect Julian and Liberty from private school or indulge in a little gentle shopping at Brent Cross.

Early or not, he thought he'd go to lunch.

The Cook Shop was on the corner of Fortess Road and Raveley Street, a godsend to someone like Kiley who appreciated good, strong coffee or a tasty soup and sandwich combo, and which, apart from term time mornings when it tended to be hysterical with young mums from the local primary school, was pretty well guaranteed to be restful and uncrowded.

'The usual?' Andrew said, turning towards the coffee machine as Kiley entered.

'Soup, I think,' Kiley said.

Eyebrow raised, Andrew glanced towards the clock. 'Suit yourself.'

Today it was mushroom and potato, helped along with a few chunks of pale rye bread. Someone had left a newspaper behind and Kiley leafed through it as he ate. Former Labour Education Minister takes her child out of the state system because his needs will be better served elsewhere. Greater transparency urged in NHS. Unseasonably warm weather along the eastern seaboard of the United States. Famous celebrity Kiley had barely heard of walks out of Big Brother house in high dudgeon.

An item on the news page caught his eye, down near the bottom of page six.

Roadside bomb kills British soldier on Basra patrol …
The death of the soldier, whose name was not immediately released, brought the number of British military fatalities in Iraq since the invasion of 2003 to 130.

Iraq, Afghanistan — maybe some day soon, Iran.

Kiley pushed the paper aside, used his last piece of bread to wipe around the inside of the bowl, slipped some coins onto the counter, and walked out into the street. Not sunbathing weather exactly, but mild for the time of year. The few greyish clouds moving slowly across the sky didn't seem to threaten rain. When he got back to his office, Jennie was sitting on the stairs; he didn't recognise her straight off and when he did he couldn't immediately recall her name.

'You don't remember me, do you?'

'Of course I do.'

'Really?' A smile crinkled the skin around her grey-green eyes and he knew her then.

'Jennie,' he said. 'Jennie Calder.'

Her hair, grown back to shoulder-length, was the same reddish shade as before.

Jennie's smile broadened. 'You do remember.'

The last time Kiley had seen her she had been standing, newly crop-haired, cigarette in hand, outside a massage parlour on Crouch End Hill, ready to go to work. Two years back, give or take.

'How's your little girl?'

'Alice? Not so little.'

'I suppose not.'

'She's at school. Nursery.'

Kiley nodded. Alice had been clinging to her mother, screaming, wide-eyed, when he had last seen her, watching as Kiley set about the two men who'd been sent by Jennie's former partner to terrorise them, mother and daughter both. Armed with a length of two-by-four and a sense of righteous indignation, he had struck hard first and left the questions for later. Some men, he'd learned, you could best reason with when they were on their knees.

'How did you find me?' he asked.

'Yellow pages.' Jennie grinned. 'Let my fingers do the walking.'

She was what, Kiley wondered, early thirties? No more. Careful make-up, more careful than before; slimmer, too: black trousers with a flare and a grey and white top beneath a long burgundy cardigan, left unfastened.

'You'd best come in.'

The main room of the second floor flat served as living room and office both: a wooden desk rescued from a skip pushed into service by the window; a swivel chair, second-hand, bought cheap from the office suppliers on Brecknock Road; a metal shelf unit and filing cabinet he'd ferried over from his previous quarters in Belsize Park. For comfort there was an easy chair that had long since shaped itself around him. A few books, directories; computer, fax and answer phone. A Bose Radio/CD player with an eclectic selection of music alongside: Ronnie

Lane, Martha Redbone, Mose Allison, Cannonball Adderley, the new Bob Dylan, old Rolling Stones.

One door led into a small kitchen, another into a shower room and lavatory and, beyond that, a bedroom which took, just, a four foot bed, a chest of drawers and a metal rail from which he hung his clothes.

Home, of a kind.

'You haven't been here long,' Jennie said.

'Observation or have you been asking around?'

Jennie smiled. 'I spoke to the bloke in the charity shop downstairs.'

'A couple of months,' Kiley said. 'The rent on the other place...' He shrugged. 'Can I get you something? Tea? Coffee? I think there's some juice.'

She shook her head. 'No, I'm fine.'

'This isn't a social call.'

'Not exactly.'

Kiley sat on one corner of his desk and waved Jennie towards the easy chair. 'Fire away.'

A heavy lorry went past outside, heading for the Great North Road, and the windows shook.

The Great North Road, Kiley thought, when had he last heard someone call it that? Seven years in the Met, four in uniform, the remainder in plain clothes; two years of professional soccer and the rest spent scuffling a living as some kind of private investigator. All the while living here or here abouts. The Great North Road — maybe it was time he took it himself. He'd been in that part of London for too long.

'This woman,' Jennie said, 'Mary. Mary Anderson. Lives near me. The flats, you know. She used to look after Alice before she started nursery. Just mornings. Alice loved her. Still does. Calls her gran. She's got this son, Terry. In the Army. Queen's Royal something-or-other, I think it is.'

'Lancers,' Kiley offered.

'That's it. Queen's Royal Lancers. They were out in Iraq. Till — what? — a month ago, something like that. End of last week, he should have gone back.'

'Iraq?'

'I don't know. Yes, I think so. But not, you know, straight off.'

'Report to the barracks first.'

Jennie nodded. 'Yes.'

'And that's what he didn't do?'

She nodded again.

'AWOL.'

Jennie blinked.

'Absent without leave.'

'Yes.'

'Does she know where he is? His mum.'

'All this last week he was staying with her, her flat. Thursday morning, that's when he was due to go back. All his kit there ready in the hall, wearing the uniform she'd ironed for him the night before. He just didn't go. Stood there, not saying anything. Ages, Mary said. Hours. Then he went back into the spare room, where he'd been sleeping and just sat there, staring at the wall. Mary, she had to go out later, mid-morning, not long, just to the shops. When she got back, he'd gone.'

'She's no idea where?'

'No. There was no note, nothing. First, of course, she thought he'd changed his mind. Gone back after all. Then she saw all his stuff, his bag and that, all dumped down beside the bed. 'Cept his uniform. He'd kept his uniform. And his gun.'

Kiley looked at her sharply.

'Mary had seen it, this rifle. Seen him cleaning it. She searched through everything but it wasn't there. He must have took it with him.'

'She's phoned the barracks to make sure …'

'They phoned her. When he didn't show. They'd got her number, next of kin. She did her best to put them off, told them he'd been taken ill. Promised to get back in touch.' Jennie shook her head. 'She's worried sick.'

'He's what? Twenty? Twenty-one?'

Jennie shook her head. 'No, that's it. He's not some kid. Thirty-five if he's a day. Sergeant, too. The army, it's a career for him. Mary says it's the only thing he's ever wanted to do.'

'All the more reason to think he'll turn up eventually. Come to his senses.'

Jennie was twisting a silver ring, round and round on her little finger. 'She said, Mary, before this happened, he'd been acting strange.'

'In what way?'

'You'd best ask her.'

'Look, I didn't say …'

'Just talk to her …'

'What for?'

'Jack…'

'What?'

'Talk to her, come on. What's the harm?'

Kiley sighed and eased his chair back from the desk. The man in the charity shop below was sorting through his collection of vinyl. The strains of some group Kiley vaguely remembered from his childhood filtered up through the board. The Easybeats? The Honeycombs? He could see why people would want to get rid of the stuff, but not why anyone would want to buy it again — not even for charity.

Jennie was still looking at him.

'How did you get here?' Kiley asked. 'Drive?'

'Walked. Suicide Bridge.'

Kiley reached for the phone. 'Let's not tempt fate twice. I'll get a cab.'

When the council named the roads on the estate after streets in New Orleans they couldn't have known about Hurricane Katrina or its aftermath. Nonetheless, following Jennie through the dog shit and debris and up onto the concrete walkway, Kiley heard inside his head, not the booming hip-hop bass or the occasional metallic shrill of electro-funk that filtered here and there through the open windows, but Dylan's parched voice singing "The Levee's Gonna Break."

Mary Anderson's flat was in the same block as Jennie's but two storeys higher, coping missing at irregular intervals from the balcony, the adjacent property boarded up. A rubber mat outside the front door read *Welcome*, the area immediately around swept and cleaned that morning, possibly scrubbed. A small vase of plastic flowers was visible through the kitchen window.

Mary Anderson herself was no more than five three or four and slightly built, her neat grey hair and flowered apron making her look older than she probably was.

'This is Jack Kiley,' Jennie said. 'The man I spoke to you about, remember? He's going to help find Terry.'

Kiley shot her a look which she ignored.

'Of course,' Mary said. 'Come in.' She held out her hand. 'Jennie, you know where to go, love. I'll just pop the kettle on.' Despite the cheeriness in her voice, there were tears ready at the corners of her eyes.

They sat in the lavender living room, cups of tea none of them really wanted in their hands, doing their best not to stare at the pictures of Terry Anderson that lined the walls. Terry in the park somewhere, three or four, pointing at the camera with a plastic gun; a school photograph in faded colour, tie askew; Terry and his dad on a shingle beach with bat and ball; a young teenager in cadet uniform, smart on parade. Others, older, head up and shoulders back, a different uniform, recognisable still as the little lad with the plastic gun. Bang, bang, you're dead.

On the mantelpiece, in a silver frame, was a carefully posed shot of Terry on his wedding day — in uniform again and with a tallish brunette in white hanging on his arm, her eyes bright and hopeful, confetti in her hair.

Arranged at either side were pictures of two young children, boy and girl, Terry's own children presumably, Mary's grandchildren.

Jennie's cup rattled against its saucer, the small noise loud in the otherwise silent room.

'You've heard nothing from him?' Kiley said.

'Nothing.'

'Not since Thursday?'

'Not a thing.'

'And you've no idea... ?'

She was already shaking her head.

'His family...' Kiley began, a nod towards the photographs.

'They separated, split up, eighteen months ago. Just after young Keiron's fifth birthday. That's him there. And Billie. I always thought it a funny name for a girl, not quite right, but she insisted...'

'Could he have gone there? To see them?'

'Him and Rebecca, they've scarce spoken. Not since it happened.'

'Even so...'

'He's not allowed. Not allowed. It makes my

blood boil. His own children and the only time he gets to see them it's an hour in some poky little room with Social Services outside the bloody door.' Her voice wobbled and Kiley thought she was going to break down and surrender to tears, but she rallied and her fingers tightened into fists, clenched in her lap.

'You've been in touch all the same?' Kiley said. 'With Rebecca, is it? To be certain.'

'I have not.'

'But…'

'Terry'd not have gone there. Not to her. A clean break, that's what she said. Better for the children. Easier all round.' She sniffed. 'Better for the children. Cutting them off from their own father. It's not natural.'

She looked at him sternly, as if defying him to say she was wrong.

'How about the children?' Kiley asked. 'Do you get to see them at all.'

'Just once since she moved away. This Christmas past. They were staying with her parents, Hertfordshire somewhere. Her parents, that's different. That's all right.' Anger made her voice tremble. "We can't stop long," she said, Rebecca, almost before I could close the door. And then she sat there where you are now, going on and on about how her parents were helping her with the rent on a new house and how they were all making a fresh start and she'd be going back to college now that she'd arranged day care. And the children sitting on the floor all the time, too scared to speak, poor lambs. Threatened with the Lord know what, I dare say, if they weren't on their best behaviour. Little Billie, she came up to me just as they were going, and whispered, "I love you, Gran," and I hugged her and said, "I love you, too. Both of you." And then she hustled them out the door.'

Kiley reached his cup from the floor. 'Terry, he knows where her parents live? Hertford-shire, you said.'

'I suppose he might.'

'You don't think Rebecca and the children might still be there?'

'I don't think so.'

'All the same, if you had an address…'

'I should have it somewhere.'

'Later will do.'

'No trouble, I'll get it now.'

'Let me,' Jennie said.

With a small sigh, Mary pushed herself up from the chair. 'I'm not an invalid yet, you know.'

She came back with a small diary, a number of addresses pencilled into the back in a shaky hand. 'There, that's them. Harpenden.'

Kiley nodded. 'And this,' he said, pointing, 'that's where Rebecca lives now?'

A brief nod. West Bridgford, Nottingham. He doubted if Rebecca had joined the ranks of disheartened County supporters just yet.

'Thanks,' he said, finishing copying the details into his notebook and passing back the diary.

'A waste of time, though,' Mary said, defiantly. 'That's not where he'll be.'

Kiley nodded. Why was it mothers insisted on knowing their sons better than anyone, evidence to the contrary? He remembered his own mother — 'Jack, I know you better than you know yourself.' Occasionally, she'd been right; more often than not so wide of the mark it had driven him into a frenzy.

His gaze turned to the pictures on the wall. 'Terry's father...'

'Cancer,' Mary said. 'Four years ago this March.' She gave a slow shake of the head. 'At least he didn't live to see this.'

After a moment, Jennie got to her feet. 'I'll make a fresh pot of tea.'

Further along the balcony a door slammed, followed by the sounds of a small dog, excited, yelping, and children's high-pitched voices; from somewhere else the whine of a drill, someone's television, voices raised in anger.

Kiley leaned forward, the movement focussing Mary's attention. 'Jennie said your son had been acting, well, a bit strangely...'

He waited. The older woman plaited her fingers slowly in and out, while, out of sight, Jennie busied herself in the kitchen.

'He couldn't sleep,' she said eventually. 'All the time he was here, I don't think he had one decent night's sleep. I'd get up sometimes to go to the lavatory, it didn't matter what time, and he'd be sitting there, in the dark, or standing over by the window, staring down. And then once, the one time he wasn't here, I was, well, surprised. Pleased. That he was sleeping at last. I tiptoed over and eased open the door to his room, just a crack. Wanted to see him, peaceful.' Her fingers stilled, then tightened. 'He was cross-legged on top of the bed, stark naked, staring. Staring right at me. As if, somehow he'd been waiting. And that gun of his, his rifle, he had it right there with him. Pointing. I shut the door as fast as I could. I might have screamed or shouted, I don't know. I just stood there, leaning back, my eyes shut tight. I couldn't move. And my heart, I could feel my heart, here, thumping hard against my chest.'

Slowly, she released her hands and smoothed her apron along her lap. Jennie was standing in the doorway, silent, listening.

'I don't know how long I stayed there. Ages it seemed. Then I went back to my room. I didn't know what else to do. I lay down but, of course, I couldn't sleep, just tossing and turning. And when I asked him, in the morning, what kind of a night he'd had, he just smiled and said, "All right, mum, you know. Not too bad. Not too bad at all." And drank his tea.'

Jennie stepped forward and rested her hands on the older woman's shoulders.

'You will find him, won't you?' Mary said. 'You'll try. Before he does something. Before something happens.'

What was he supposed to say?

'What do you think?' Jennie asked.

They were walking along the disused railway line that ran east from Crouch Hill towards Finsbury Park, grassed over now to make an urban footpath, the grass itself giving way to mud and gravel, the sides a dumping ground for broken bicycles and bundles of free newspapers no one could be bothered to deliver.

'I think he's taken a lot of stress,' Kiley said. 'Seen things most of us wouldn't even like to consider. But if he stays away there's always the risk of arrest, dishonourable discharge. Even prison. My best guess, he'll get himself to a doctor before it's too late, take whatever time he needs, report back with a medical certificate and a cart load of pills. That way, with any luck he might even hang on to his pension.'

'And if none of that happens?'

A blackbird startled up from the under-growth to their left and settled again on the branches of a bush a little further along.

'People go missing all the time.'

'People with guns?'

Kiley shortened his stride. 'I'll go out to Harpenden first, make sure they're not still there. Terry could have been in touch, doing the same thing.'

'I met her once,' Jennie said. 'Rebecca.' She made a face. 'Sour as four-day old milk.'

Kiley grinned. They walked on, saying little, just comfortable enough in each other's company without feeling really at ease, uncertain how far to keep walking, when to stop and turn back.

The house was to the north of the town, take a left past the golf club and keep on going; find yourself in Batford, you've gone too far. Of course, he could have done the whole thing on the phone, but in these days of so much cold calling, conversations out of the blue were less than welcome. And Kiley was attuned to sniffing around; accustomed, where possible, to seeing the whites of their eyes. How else could you hope to tell if people were lying?

The house sat back, smug, behind a few straggly poplars and a lawn with too much moss in it for its own good. A mud-splashed four-wheel drive sat off to one side, the space in front of the double garage taken up by a fair-sized boat secured to a trailer. How far in God's name, Kiley wondered, were they from the sea?

The door bell played something that sounded to Kiley as if it might be by Puccini, but if he were expecting the door itself to be opened by a Filipino maid in a starched uniform or even a grim-faced au pair, he was mistaken. The woman appraising him was clearly the lady of the house, a fit-looking fiftyish with a fine tan and her hair swept up into what Kiley thought might be called a French roll — or was that twist? She was wearing cream trousers, snug at the hips, and a grey marl sweater with a high collar. There were rings on most of her fingers.

'Mr Kiley?'

Kiley nodded.

'You're very prompt.'

If he were a dog, Kiley thought, she would be offering him a little treat for being good. Instead she held out her hand.

'Christina Hadfield.'

Beneath the smoothness of her skin, her grip was sure and firm.

'Please come in. I'm afraid my husband's not here. Some business or other.'

As he followed her through a square hallway busy with barbour jackets, green wellingtons and walking boots, the lines from one of his favourite Mose Alison songs came to mind.

I know her daddy got some money
I can tell by the way she walks

The room they went into sported two oversized settees and a small convention of easy chairs and you could have slotted in most of Mary Anderson's flat with space to spare. High windows looked out into the garden, where someone, out of sight, was whistling softly as he — or she — tidied away the leaves. Presumably not Mr. H.

Photographs of the two grandchildren, more recent than those on Mary Anderson's wall, stood, silver-framed, on the closed lid of a small piano.

'They're adorable,' she said, following his stare. 'Perfectly sweet. And well-behaved. Which is more than you can say for the majority of children nowadays.' She pursed her lips together. 'Discipline in our society, I'm afraid, has become a dirty word.'

'How long did they stay?' Kiley asked.

'A little over a week. Long enough to help undress the tree, take down the decorations.' Christina Hadfield smiled. 'Twelfth night. Another old tradition gone begging.'

'Terry, their father, he was home on leave while they were here.'

'If you say so.'

'He didn't make any kind of contact?'

'Certainly not.'

'No phone calls, no…'

'He knows better than to do that after what happened.'

'What did happen?'

'When Rebecca first said she was leaving him he refused to believe her. And then when he did, he became violent.'

'He hit her?'

'He threatened to. Threatened her and the children with all manner of things. She called in the police.'

'He was back in England then, when she told him?'

'My daughter is not a coward, Mr Kiley, whatever else. Foolish, I grant you. Slow to acknowledge her mistakes.' Reaching down towards the low table beside her chair, she offered Kiley a cigarette and when he shook his head, lit one for herself, holding down the smoke before letting it drift up towards the ceiling. 'What possessed her to marry that man I was always at a loss to understand, and unfortunately, circumstances proved my reservations correct. It was a mismatch from the start. And a shame it took the best part of four years in non-commissioned quarters — bad plumbing and condensation streaming down the walls — to bring her to her senses.'

'That's why she left him? For a better class of accommodation?'

Christina Hadfield's mouth tightened. 'She left him because she wanted a better life for her children. As any mother would.'

'His children, too, surely?'

'Is that what you're here for? To be his apologist? To plead his cause?'

'I explained when I called…'

'What you gave me to understand on the telephone was that the unfortunate man was having some kind of a breakdown. To the extent that he might do himself some harm.'

'I think it's possible. I'd like to find him before anything like that happens.'

'In this, you're acting for his mother?'

'Yes.'

'Poor woman.' Smoke drifted from the

corners of her mouth. 'After speaking to you, I telephoned Rebecca. As I suspected she's heard nothing from him. Certainly not recently.'

'I see.' Kiley got to his feet. Whoever had been whistling while they worked outside had fallen silent. Christina Hadfield's gaze was unwavering. What must it be like, Kiley thought, to entertain so little doubt? He took a card from his pocket and set it on the table. 'Should Terry get in touch or should your daughter hear from him... Unlikely as that might be.'

No call to shake hands again at the door. She stood for a few moments, arms folded, watching him go, making good and sure he left the premises.

Was it the fact that his grandfather — his father's father — had been an engine driver that left Kiley so susceptible to trains? The old man — that was how he had always seemed to Kiley, though he could not have been a good deal older than Kiley himself was now — had worked on the old London and Midland

Railway, the LMS, and, later, the LNER. Express trains to Leeds and Newcastle, smuts forever blackening his face and hair. Kiley could see him, home at the end of a lengthy shift, standing by the range in their small kitchen, sipping Camp coffee from the saucer. Rarely speaking.

Now, Kiley, who didn't own a car, and hired one from the local pay-as-you-go scheme when necessary, travelled by train whenever possible. A window seat in the quiet coach, a book to read, his CD Walkman turned low.

His relationship with Kate, a freelance journalist whom he had met when working security at an Iranian Film Festival on the South Bank and who, after some eighteen months, had cast him aside in favour of an earnest video installation artist, had left him, a sore heart and a taste for wine beyond his income aside, with a thing for reading. Some of the stuff that Kate had offloaded on him he couldn't handle — Philip Roth, Zadie Smith, Ian McEwan — while others — Graham Greene, the Chandlers she'd given him as a half-assed joke about his profession,

Annie Proulx — he'd taken to easily. Jim Harrison, he'd found on his own. The charity shop below his office, where he'd also discovered Hemingway — a dog-eared Penguin paperback of *To Have and Have Not* with the cover half torn away. Thomas McGuane.

What he was reading now was *The Man Who Liked Slow Tomatoes*, which, when he'd been scanning the shelves in Kentish Town Oxfam, he'd first taken for yet another celebrity cookery book, but which had turned out to be an odd kind of crime novel about Mario Balzic, an ageing cop trying to hold things together in a dying industrial town in Pennsylvania. So far, more than half the book was in dialogue, a lot of which Kiley didn't fully understand, but somehow that didn't seem to matter.

For a few moments, he set the book aside and gazed out of the window. They were just north of Bedford, he guessed, the train gathering speed, and most of the low mist that had earlier been clinging to the hedgerows and rolling out across the sloping fields had disappeared. Off to the east, beyond a bank of threadbare trees, the sun was slowly breaking through. Turning down the Walkman a touch more, Mose Allison's trumpet quietly essaying *Trouble in Mind*, he reopened his book and began chapter thirteen.

Nottingham station, when they arrived, was moderately busy, anonymous and slightly scruffy. The young Asian taxi driver seemed to know where Kiley wanted to go.

Travelling along London Road, he saw the floodlights of the County ground where he had once played. Had it been just the once? He thought it was. Then they were crossing the River Trent with the Forest pitch away to their left — the Brian Clough stand facing towards him — and, almost immediately, passing the high rows of white seats at one end of Trent Bridge, where, in a rare moment of recent glory, the English cricket team had sent the Australians packing.

It was a short street of smallish houses off the Melton Road, the number he was looking for at the far end on the left, a flat-fronted two-storey terraced house with only flaking paint work to distinguish it from those on either side.

The bell didn't seem to be working and after a couple of tries he knocked instead. A flier for the local pizza parlour was half-in half-out of the letter box and, pulling it clear, he bent down and peered through. Nothing moved. When he called, 'Hello!', his voice echoed tinnily back. Crouching there, eyes growing accustomed to the lack of light inside, he could just make out a toy dog, left stranded, splay-legged, in the middle of the narrow hall.

'I think they're away,' a woman's voice said.

She was standing at the open doorway of the house alongside. Sixties, possibly older, spectacles, yellow duster in hand. The floral apron, Kiley thought, must be making a comeback.

'Most often I can hear the kiddies of a morning.' She shook her head. 'Not today. Quiet as the grave.'

'You don't know where they might have gone?'

'No idea, duck. You here for the meter or what?'

Kiley shook his head. 'Friend of a friend. Just

called round on the off chance, really.'

The woman nodded.

'She didn't say anything to you?' Kiley asked. 'About going away?'

'Not to me. Keeps herself to herself, mostly. Not unfriendly, but you know…'

'You didn't see her leaving? Her and the children?'

'Can't say as I did.'

'And there hasn't been anybody else hanging round? A man?'

'Look, what is this? Are you the police or what?'

Kiley tried for a reassuring smile. 'Nothing like that. Nothing to worry about.'

'Well, you could try next door the other side, they might know something. Or the fruit and veg shop back on Melton Road, I've seen her in there a time or two, chatting like.'

Kiley thanked her and rang the next door bell but there was no one home. Between serving customers, the fruit and veg man was happy enough to pass the time of day, but could provide nothing in the way of useful information.

There was a narrow alley running down behind the houses, mostly taken up with green wheelie bins; a low gate gave access to a small, square yard. The rear curtains were pulled part way across.

Through the glass Kiley could see the remains of a sliced loaf, left unwrapped beside the sink; a tub of Flora with no lid; a pot of jam; a wedge of cheese, unwrapped. A child's coat lay bunched on the floor; a chair on its side by the far wall. Signs of unseemly haste.

The back door seemed not to be sitting snug in its frame. When Kiley applied pressure with the flat of his hand it gave a few millimetres, loose on its hinges, rattled, then stuck. No key, Kiley guessed, turned in the lock, but bolted at the top. A swift kick would have it open.

He hesitated, uncertain what to do.

Dave Prentiss's number was in his mobile; Prentiss, whom he'd worked with as a young DC when he'd first made it into plain clothes, and now in line for commander.

'Dave? Hi! It's Jack. Jack Kiley... No, fine, thanks. Yes, grand... Listen, Dave, you don't happen to know anyone up in Nottingham, do you? Someone you've worked with, maybe. Might be willing to give me the time of day?'

Resnick had been up since before five, Lynn heading up some high power surveillance and needing to be in place to supervise the changeover, a major drugs supplier their target and kudos all round if they could pull it off. Resnick had made them both coffee, toast for himself, a rye loaf he'd picked up on the way home the day before, Lynn crunching her way through Dorset muesli with skimmed milk and a sliced banana.

'Why don't you go back to bed?' she'd said. 'Get another couple of hours.'

She'd kissed him at the door, the morning air cold against her cheek.

'You take care,' he'd said.

'You too.'

One of the cats wandered in from outside, sampled an early breakfast and, despite the presence of a cat flap, miaowed to be let out again.

Instead of taking Lynn's advice, Resnick readied the smaller stove top pot and made himself fresh coffee. Easing back the curtains in the living room, the outside still dark, he sat thumbing through the previous night's *Evening Post,* listening to Lester Young. Would he rather have been out there where Lynn was, the heart of the action, so called? Until recently, yes. Now, with possible retirement tapping him on the shoulder, he was less sure.

He was at his desk by eight, nevertheless, breaking the back of the paperwork before it broke him. Dave Prentiss rang a little after eleven and they passed a pleasant enough ten minutes, mostly mulling over old times. There was a lot of that these days, Resnick thought.

At a quarter to twelve, an officer called up from reception to say a Jack Kiley was there to see him. He got to his feet as Kiley entered, extending his hand.

'Jack.'

'Detective Inspector.'

'Charlie.'

'Okay, then. Charlie.'

The two men looked at one another. They were of similar height, but with Resnick a good stone and half heavier, the buttons on his blue shirt straining above his belt. Both still had a fullish head of hair, Resnick's darker and, if anything, a little thicker. Kiley, thinner-faced and a good half-a-dozen years younger, had a leaner, more athletic build. Resnick, in contrast, had the slightly weary air of a man who has spent too long sitting in the same comfortable chair. Balzic, Kiley thought for a moment, harking back to the book he'd been reading, Mario Balzic.

'Dave Prentiss said you might need a favour,' Resnick said.

'You could call it that.'

Resnick gestured towards a chair. 'Better sit.'

Kiley gave him a succinct version of events, what he knew, what he feared.

'You think they might be inside?'

'I think it's possible.'

Resnick nodded. There had been a case not too long ago, north of the city. A man who'd discovered his wife was having an affair with a colleague and was planning to leave him; he had smothered two of the children with a pillow, smashed their mother's head open with a hammer and left her bleeding on the kitchen floor. The police had found a third child hiding in the airing cupboard, limbs locked in fear.

There were other instances, too.

Almost a commonplace.

'You say the back door's only bolted?'

'So it seems.'

'You didn't go in yourself?'

'I thought about it. Thought it might not be such a great idea.'

Resnick considered, then reached towards the phone. 'I'll organise a car.'

'This could be a wild goose chase,' Kiley said as they were descending the stairs.

'Let's hope, eh?'

The driver was fresh-faced, carrot-haired, barely out of training. They're not only getting younger, Kiley thought, this one can only just see over the top of the steering wheel.

In the back of the car, Resnick was studying Kiley intently. 'Charlton Athletic, wasn't it?' he said eventually.

Grinning, Kiley nodded.

'Cup game down at Meadow Lane,' Resnick said.

Another nod.

'90/91.'

'Yes.'

'A good season for us.'

'You had a good team.'

'Tommy Johnson.'

'Mark Draper.'

Resnick smiled, remembering.

'Good Cup year for you, wasn't it?'

'Through to the Sixth Round. Spurs beat us 2-1 at White Hart Lane.'

'We should've stopped you sooner.'

'You had your chances.'

Kiley looked out through the window. Off licence. Estate agent. Delicatessen. He had spent most of the game on the bench and only been sent on for the last fifteen minutes. Before he could adjust to the pace, the ball had come to him on the edge of the area and, with the centre half closing in on him, he had let fly and, leaning back too far, his shot had ballooned over the bar. Then, a goal down and with less than five minutes to spare, he had nicked the ball away from the full back, cut inside, and, with only the goalie to beat, had skewed it wide. At the final whistle he had turned away disgusted as the Notts players ran towards their fans in triumph.

'All a long time ago,' Resnick said. 'Fifteen years.'

'And the rest.'

'Think about it much?'

Kiley shook his head. 'Hardly at all.'

The car swung round into Manvers Road and they were there. Still no one was answering the door. Round at the back, Resnick hesitated only a moment before putting his shoulder to the door, once, twice, before the bolt snapped free. He stepped carefully into the kitchen, Kiley following. Nothing had been moved. The cloth dog, two shades of brown, still sat, neglected, in the hall. The front room was empty and they turned back towards the stairs. A chill spread down the backs of Resnick's legs and along his arms. The stairs creaked a little beneath his weight. A child's blue cardigan lay, discarded, on the landing. The door to the main bedroom was closed.

Drawing a slow breath, Resnick turned the handle. The bed had been hastily made; the wardrobe doors stood open and several garments had slid from their hangers to the floor. There was no one there.

They turned back towards the other room, its door ajar.

The closer of the two, Kiley looked round at Resnick enquiringly then nudged the door wide.

There were bunk beds against the right hand wall. Posters on the wall, a white melamine set of drawers. Several clear plastic boxes, stacked on top of one another, filled with toys. Stuffed animals and pieces of Lego and picture books strewn across the floor.

Kiley felt the muscles in his stomach relax. 'They're not here.'

'Thank God for that.'

Back downstairs they stood in the kitchen, Resnick taking in the evidence of hasty sandwich making, the fallen chair.

There were a dozen explanations, mostly harmless, some more plausible than the rest. 'You think they've done a runner?' he said.

'I think they might have tried.'

'And if they didn't succeed?'

Kiley released a long, slow breath. 'Then he's taken them, that's what I'd say.'

'Against their will?'

'Odds are.'

Resnick called the station from the car; arranged for the place to be secured and scene of crime officers to attend. Jumping to conclusions they might be, but better that than to do nothing and wait for bad news.

***

Terry Anderson had waited, cautious, van parked just around the corner on Exchange Road, back towards the primary school. From there he could see the house, see if Rebecca had any callers, visitors in or out, make sure the coast was clear. Waiting. Watching. Alert. Ready for danger, the least sign. It was nothing to him. What he was trained for. Northern Ireland. Iraq. Afghanistan. Belfast. Basra. Sangin. Someone waiting to take your head off with a rifle or blow you to buggery with an RPG.

Little happened. The occasional couple returning home from visiting friends, an hour in the pub, an evening in town. Men taking their dogs for a last walk around the block, pausing perhaps, to light a cigarette. Television screens flickering brightly between half-closed blinds. House lights going on, going off.

He sat behind the front seats, leaning back, legs stretched in front of him, out of sight to passers by. Beside him in the van were blankets, sleeping bags, bottles of water. A few basic supplies. First aid kit. Ammunition. Tools. Tinned food. His uniform, folded neatly. Waterproofs. Rope. Prepared.

As he watched, the downstairs room of Rebecca's house went suddenly dark and he imagined, rather than heard, the sound some moments later as she turned the key in the front door lock. Careful, he liked that. Not careful enough.

Eleven thirty-five.

She'd been watching, he guessed, a re-run of some American soap or a late night film and had either got bored or found her eyes closing, unbidden. How many times had they sat together like that in the semi-dark, the change in her breathing alerting him to the fact that she had dropped off, unwillingly, to sleep? Her warm breath when he had leaned over to kiss her, her head turning away.

The upstairs light went on and, for a brief moment, he saw her in silhouette, standing there, looking out, looking down; then the curtains were pulled across, leaving a faint yellowish glow.

Automatically, he rechecked his watch.

Imagined the children, already sleeping.

The houses to either side had gone dark long since, but up and down the street there were still signs of life.

He would wait.

***

That night, Rebecca stirred, wondering if she had ever really been asleep and, if so, for how long? The bedside clock read 01:14. It was her bladder that had awoken her and, grudgingly, she slid her legs round from beneath the duvet and touched her feet to the carpeted floor. The house was smaller than she might have liked, and at times, even for the three of them, barely large enough — bedlam when one or more of Keiron's friends came round after school to play. But the fixtures and fittings were in better nick than in many of the other places she'd seen and the rent, with her parents' help, was reasonable enough. If it weren't for them, she didn't know what she could have done.

Careful not to flush the toilet for fear of waking Billie — a light sleeper at best — she eased back the door and slipped into their room. Keiron's thumb was in his mouth and carefully she prised it free, causing him to grunt and turn his head sharply to one side, but not to wake. Billie, pink pyjama top gathered at her neck, was clinging to edge of the blanket she had slept with since she was three months old.

Straightening, Rebecca shivered as if — what did her grandmother used to say? — as if someone had just walked over her grave.

Rubbing her arms beneath the sleeves of the long T-shirt she was wearing, she turned and went softly back to bed, this time, hopefully, to sleep through. The morning would come soon enough.

When she woke again it had just gone two. Levering herself up on to one elbow, she strained to hear. Had one of the children woken and cried out? A dream, perhaps? Or maybe Keiron had got up and gone to the toilet on his own?

No, it was nothing.

The wind, perhaps, rattling the window panes.

Her head had barely touched the pillow, when she heard it again, for certain this time, the sound that had awoken her, a footstep. Next door, it had to be next door. Quite often, late at night, she heard them moving. Early, too. Her breath caught in her throat. No. There was somebody in the house, somebody down below, a footstep on the stairs.

Rebecca froze.

If I close my eyes, will it go away?

It.

He.

Whoever…

For the first time she wanted a phone beside the bed, a panic button, something. With a lunge, she threw back the covers and sprang from the bed. Three, four steps and she was at the door and reaching for the light.

Oh, Christ!

The figure of a man, turning at the stop of the stairs.

Christ!

Her hand stifled a scream.

'It's all right,' the voice said. 'It's all right.' A voice she recognised, reassuring, commanding.

'Terry?'

He continued slowly towards her, his face still in shadow.

'Terry?'

'Who else?' Almost smiling. 'Who else?'

With a sob, she sank to her knees, and he

reached down and touched her hair, uncertainly at first, easing her head forward until it rested against his body, one of her hands clinging to his leg, the other pressed hard against the floor.

They stood in the bedroom, Rebecca with a cotton dressing gown pulled hastily round her. She had stopped shaking, but her breathing was still unsteady. He was wearing a black roll-neck sweater, camouflage trousers, black army boots.

'What are you... What are you doing?'

When he smiled, nothing changed in his eyes. 'Terry, what...'

'Get the children.'

'What?'

'Get yourself dressed and then get the children.'

'No, you can't...'

When he reached towards her, she flinched.

'Just something sensible, jeans. Nothing fancy. Them the same.'

She waited until he turned away.

'Keiron and Billie, they're in back, are they?'

'Yes, but let me go first, you'll frighten them.'

'No, it's okay. You get on.'

'Terry, no…'

'Get on.'

'You won't…'

He looked at her then. 'Hurt them?'

'Yes.'

He shook his head. 'They're my kids, aren't they?'

Billie was awake when he got to the door and when he moved closer towards her she screamed. Rebecca, half-dressed, came running, brushed past him and took the three year old into her arms. 'It's all right, sweetheart, it's only daddy.'

She sobbed against Rebecca's shoulder.

On the top bunk, Keiron stirred, blinking towards the landing light. 'Dad?'

Fingers and thumbs, Rebecca helped them into their clothes, Keiron with a school sweat shirt pulled down over his Forest top, Billie snapped into her blue dungarees.

'Where we going, mum?' Keiron asked.

'I'm not sure, love.'

'An adventure,' his father said, coming through the door. 'We're going on an adventure.'

'Really?'

'You bet!' He tousled the boy's hair.

'You mean like camping?'

'Yes, a bit like that.'

'Like you in the army.'

'Yes. Like that.'

'Some of the year sixes go camping overnight. Cook their own food and everything. Can we do that?'

'Prob'ly, we'll see.'

'And take a pack-up? Can we take a pack-up?'

'No need, son. I've got all the stuff we need.'

'But they do, carry it with them. Can't we?'

'Yes, all right, then. Why not? Becca, how about it? Like the boy says. Fix us something quick. Sandwich, anything. Go on, I'll finish up here.'

When he got down to the kitchen, a few minutes later, there were bread, a pot of jam and some cheese but no Rebecca; he found her in the front room, texting.

'The fuck!'

Before he could reach her, she'd deleted the message. Swinging her hard towards him, he snatched the phone from her hand. 'Who was that going to be to? The police? The fucking police?' He hurled the phone against the wall and, pushing her aside, crushed it with the heel of his boot. 'Now get in that kitchen and get finished. Five fucking minutes and we're leaving. Five.'

Keiron was standing, open mouthed, at the living room door and behind him somewhere Billie had started to cry.

It was early evening and they were sitting in Resnick's office, a light rain blurring the window, the intermittent snarl and hum of traffic from the street.

'Here's what we've got so far,' Resnick said. 'Two sets of adult prints in the house, one we're assuming Terry Anderson's. Looks as if he forced the lock on the back door. Not difficult. Explains why it was only bolted across. There was a mobile phone, Rebecca's, in the front room. Beneath the settee. Broken. Smashed on purpose.'

'Used recently?' Kiley asked.

'One call earlier that evening, to a friend. We've already spoken to her, nothing there.'

'No mention of going away, taking a trip?'

'Nothing.'

'And the husband? She didn't say anything about him? Being worried at all?'

Resnick shook his head. 'We've checked with the school and the nursery where she takes the little girl. Both surprised when the kids didn't turn up this morning. Nursery phoned but got no answer, assumed she'd been taken sick. School, the same.'

Kiley shifted uncomfortably on his chair.

'More luck with the neighbours,' Resnick said. 'Old lady next door, bit of a light sleeper, reckons she heard a child scream. A little after two. Either that or a fox, she couldn't be sure. Person from across the street, sleeps with the window open, thinks he might have heard a vehicle driving away, that would be later, around two thirty. There's not a lot more. A couple of people mentioned seeing a van parked in Exchange Road, just around the corner. Not usually there. Small, white, maybe a black stripe down the side. Could have been a Citroën, according to one. We're following that up, checking CCTV. That time of night, roads shouldn't be too busy. Might spot something.' He leaned back. 'Not a lot else to go on.'

'You've sent out descriptions?' Kiley said.

'As best we can. Local airports. Birmingham.'

'They could have gone with him willingly,' Kiley said.

'Is that what you think?'

'What I'd like to think,' Kiley said. 'Not the same thing.'

Keiron helped him put up the tent. The trees in that part of the forest had mostly lost their leaves, but the undergrowth was thick enough to shield them from sight. None of the regular paths came near. Tent up, they foraged for fallen branches and dragged them to the site, arranging them over the bracken. Several times, Keiron cut himself on thorns and briars, but he just sucked at the blood and bit back the tears. Big boy, trying not to be afraid.

'How long?' Rebecca wanted to ask. 'How long are we going to be here?' Reading the look on Anderson's face, she said nothing.

The sandwiches were finished quickly. Amongst the supplies he had provided were tins of corned beef and baked beans, peach slices in syrup. Biscuits. Bottles of water. Tea bags and a jar of instant coffee, though he didn't want the risk of lighting a fire. They had driven the van some way along the main track then gone the rest of the way on foot, making two journeys to carry everything. Still dark. Just the light of a single torch. Taking Keiron with him, Anderson had gone back to move the van.

Before leaving, he had taken Rebecca to one side. 'You'll be here when we get back, you and Billie. Right here. Okay?'

'Yes.' A whisper.

'I'm sorry?'

'I said, yes. Yes, all right.' Not able to look him in the eye.

'It better be.'

By the time they had returned, Keiron was exhausted, out on his feet, and his father had had to carry him the last half mile. Billie was asleep, stretched across her mother's lap. While he had been away, she had tried walking a little way in each direction, taking Billie with her, careful never to wander too far and lose her way back. She had seen nobody, heard nothing. She felt stupid for not doing anything more, without knowing what, safely, she could have done.

'You look knackered,' Anderson said. 'Tired out. Why don't you get your head down? Get a bit of sleep while you can.'

When she opened her eyes, not so many minutes later, he was sitting cross-legged at the far side of the tent, rifle close beside him, painstakingly cleaning his knife.

***

Not wanting to stand around like a spare part, waiting, Kiley had walked into the city, found a halfway decent place for breakfast and settled down to a bacon cob with brown sauce and a mug of serious tea, trying to concentrate on his book. No such luck. Jennie had rung him earlier on his mobile and he'd hesitated before giving her a truncated version of what little they knew, what they surmised.

'Don't say anything to his mother,' he'd said. 'Not yet, anyway.'

'What d'you take me for?'

'I'll call you if I know anything more definite.'

'You promise?'

Kiley had promised.

Breakfast over, he wandered around the city centre. The square in front of the council building was going through some kind of makeover; maybe they were turning it into a car park. The pavements were busy with early shoppers, people hurrying, late, to work, the occasional drinker with his can of cider clutched tight. He walked up the hill towards the Theatre Royal. Duncan Preston in *To Kill a Mockingbird*. All next week, *The Rocky Horror Show*. Big Time American Wrestling at The Royal Concert Hall. He was half way down King Street, heading back towards the square, when his mobile rang. It was Resnick. They'd found something.

There was an OS map open on the table when Kiley arrived, the blurred image of a van frozen on the computer screen. Night time. Overhead lights reflected in the road surface. There were several other officers in the room.

'Two sightings of the possible van,' Resnick said.

One of the officers, dark hair, dandruff on his shoulders, set the CCTV footage in motion.

'The first here, junction 27 of the MI, leaving the motorway and heading east towards the A608. And then here — see the time code — not so many minutes later, at the roundabout where it joins the 611. Turning south.'

'Back towards the city?' Kiley said, surprised.

'Could be,' Resnick said, 'but for my money, more likely heading here. Annesley Forest.' He was pointing at a patch of green covering almost two squares of the map.

'Why there?'

'Couple of years back, just north of here, Annesley Woodhouse, this man was found dead outside his home, ex-miner, lacerations to the head and upper body, crossbow found close by.'

'Robin bloody Hood,' someone remarked.

'According to what we heard,' Resnick continued, 'there'd been one heck of a row between the dead man and a neighbour, all harking back to the miners' strike, '84.

When we went to talk to the neighbour, of course he'd scarpered, gone to ground right there.' Resnick pointed again. 'Two and a half kilometres of woodland. Then, as if that weren't bad enough, a second man, wanted for turning a shotgun on his own daughter, went missing in the same area. Bloody nightmare. We had extra personnel drafted in from all over, round five hundred all told. Dog teams, helicopters, everything. If that's where Anderson's gone, he could stay holed up for weeks.'

'But we don't know for sure,' Kiley said

'We know next to bugger all,' one of the officers said.

Resnick silenced him with a look. 'There's forest all around,' he said, 'not just this patch here. A lot of it, though, is criss-crossed with trails, paths going right through. Sherwood Forest especially, up by the Major Oak, even at this time of the year it's pretty busy with visitors. But this is different. Quiet.'

Looking at the map, Kiley nodded. 'How sure are we about the van?' he said.

'Traced the number plate. Citroën Berlingo. Rented from a place in north London — Edgware — two days ago. Name of Terence Alderman. Alderman, Alexander, TA, close enough. Paid in cash.'

'If he's gone into the woods…' Kiley began.

'Then he'll have likely dumped the van. We've got people out looking now. Until that turns up, or we get reports of a sighting, it's still pretty much conjecture. And, as far as we know, nobody's been harmed.'

'I doubt if he's taken them for their own good.'

'Even so. I need a little more before I can order up a major search. Request one, at least.'

By which time, Kiley thought, what they were fearing but not yet saying, could already have happened.

'I thought I might take a ride out that way,' Resnick said. 'Want to come along?'

***

While Rebecca watched, Anderson had talked both children into a game of hide and seek, warning them not to stray too far. Billie giggled from the most obvious hiding places, waving her arms, as if the point of the game was to be found. Once, Keiron skinnied down inside a hollow oak and stayed there so silent that his father, fearing maybe he'd run off, had called his name in anger and the boy had only shown himself reluctantly, scared of a telling-off or worse.

They picked at the corned beef, ate biscuits and cold beans, drank the sweet syrupy peach juice straight from the cans.

'We should have done this more often,' Anderson said.

'Done what?' said Rebecca sharply.

'Gone camping,' he said and laughed.

Sitting on the ground outside the tent, he showed his son how to strip down the rifle and reassemble it again.

'Can we go after some rabbits?' Keiron asked.

'Maybe tomorrow.'

'Will we still be here tomorrow?'

He left the question unanswered.

Just out of sight, beyond some trees, Anderson had dug a latrine. Walking back, Rebecca was aware of him watching her, the movement of her body inside her clothes.

'Are you seeing anyone?' he asked.

'Seeing?'

'You know what I mean.'

'No.'

'No man then?'

'No.'

'Why not?'

'I don't know. I'm just not.'

'You should.'

She went on past him and into the tent.

**

The day was sealed in with grey. Low hedgerows and mudded tracks and the occasional ploughed field. Why was it, Kiley asked himself, they didn't seem to plough fields any more, ploughed and left bare? Londoner that he was, he could swear that was what he remembered, travelling north to visit relations in Bucks. Mile after mile of ploughed fields. That rackety little train that stopped everywhere. What was it? Hemel Hempstead, Kings Langley, Abbots Langley, Berkhamstead, Tring? His uncle, red-faced and — now, he thought, looking back — unreal, waiting outside the station at Leighton Buzzard, to take them home in a Rover that rattled more than the carriages of the train.

Resnick had opted to drive, the two of them up front as they made a careful circuit: Newstead, Papplewick pumping station, Ravenshead, south of Mansfield and back again, the A611 straight as a die from the corner of Cauldwell Wood, across Cox Moor to Robin Hood's Hill and the supposed site of Robin Hood's Cave. Then back down towards the forest, the trees at first bordering both sides of the road and then running thickly to the left.

'Do you ever miss it?' Resnick asked, out of nowhere.

It took Kiley a moment to respond. 'Playing?'

A grunt he took to mean, yes. What answer did

he want? 'Sometimes,' Kiley said. 'Once in a while.'

'Like when?'

Kiley smiled. 'Most Saturday afternoons.'

'You don't play at all?'

'Not for years. Helped a friend coach some kids for a while, that was all.'

Resnick eased down on the brake and pulled out to pass an elderly man on a bicycle, raincoat flapping in the wind, cloth cap pulled down, bottoms of his trousers tied up with string.

'Up and down this road, I shouldn't wonder,' Resnick said, 'since nineteen fifty three or thereabouts.'

Kiley smiled. 'How about you?' he said. 'County. You still go?'

'For my sins.'

'Perhaps we'll catch a game some time?'

'Perhaps.'

Resnick's phone rang and he answered, slowing to the side of the road. 'We've found the van,' he said, breaking the connection. 'Aldercar wood. No more than a mile from here. Off the main road to the left.'

It had been driven beyond the end of the track and into some trees, covered over with bracken, the inside stripped clear. The main area of forest was clearly visible across two fields, stretching north and west.

'Looks like your surmise was correct,' Kiley said.

Resnick nodded. 'Looks like.'

***

Anderson had gone silent, drawn back into himself. No more family games. Once, when Keiron had run over to him, excited about something he'd found, his father had just stared at him, blank, and the boy had backed nervously away, before running to his mother and burying his face against her chest.

Billie fretted and whined until Rebecca plaited her hair and told her the story of Sleeping Beauty yet again, the little girl's face lighting up at the moment when the princess is kissed awake. She'll learn, Rebecca thought, and hopefully before it's too late.

'How did the prince find her?' Billie asked, not for the first time.

'He cut his way through the undergrowth with his sword.'

'Perhaps someone will find us like that,' Billie said.

Rebecca glanced across at Anderson, but if he had heard he gave no sign.

A light rain had started to fall.

Without preamble, Anderson sprang to his feet and pulled on his cagoule. 'Just a walk,' he said. 'I'll not be long.'

A moment later, he was striding through the trees.

Keiron ran after him, calling; tripped and fell, ran and tripped again; finally turned and came limping towards the tent.

'He isn't coming back,' the boy said, crestfallen.

Rebecca kissed him gently on his head. 'We'll see.'

An hour passed. Two. Once Rebecca thought she heard voices and called out in their direction, but there was no reply and the voices faded away till there were just the sounds of the forest. Distant cars. An aeroplane overhead.

'I told you,' Keiron said accusingly and kicked at the ground.

'Right,' Rebecca said, making up her mind. 'Put on your coats and scarves. We're going.'

'Where? To find daddy?'

'Yes,' Rebecca lied.

Billie fussed with her buttons and when Rebecca knelt to help her, the child pushed her away. 'I can do it. I can do it myself.'

'Well, get a move on.'

'I am.' Bottom lip stuck petulantly out.

Calm down, Rebecca told herself. Calm down.

Billie pushed the last button into place.

'All right?' Rebecca said. 'Come on, then. Let's go.'

They were a hundred metres away, maybe less, heading in what Rebecca thought was the direction they'd originally come, when they saw him just a short way ahead, walking purpose-fully towards them.

'Come to meet me? That's nice.'

As the children went into the tent, he pulled

her back. 'Try that again and I'll fuckin' kill you, so help me.'

***

There were only a couple of hours of daylight left. By the time they had got a decent-sized search party organised there would be even less. Best to wait until first light.

'I've been talking to the Royal Military police,' Resnick said. 'Seems as though one sergeant going AWOL isn't too high on their list of priorities. Too many of them, apparently, done the same. Not keen on hurrying back to fight for someone else's democracy. More interested in tracking down a batch of illicit guns, smuggled into the UK from Iraq via Germany. Bit of a burgeoning trade in exchanging them for drugs and currency. Cocaine, especially. Still, they're sending someone up tomorrow. If we do find Anderson, they'll want to stake their claim.'

'Till then we twiddle our thumbs.'

'Do better than that, I dare say,' Resnick said.

Tony Burns was up from London, sitting in with a local band at The Five Ways. Geoff Pearson on bass, the usual crew. Last time Resnick had heard Burns, a good few years back, he'd been playing mostly baritone, a little alto. Now it was all tenor, a sound not too many miles this side of Stan Getz. Jake McMahon joined them for the last number, a tear-up through the chords of "Cherokee". By now the free cobs were going round, end of the evening, cheese or ham, and Kiley was having a pretty good time.

Resnick had called Lynn and asked her if she wanted to join them, but instead she had opted for an early night. She'd left him a note on the kitchen table, signed with love.

Resnick made coffee and, feeling expansive, cracked open a bottle of Highland Park. They sat listening to Ben Webster and Art Tatum and then Monk fingering his way through "Between the Devil and the Deep Blue Sea", Kiley not without envy for what seemed, in some respects, a fuller, more comfortable life than his own.

'Well,' said Resnick, finally, levering himself

up from his chair. 'Early start.'

'You bet.'

The bed was made up in the spare room, a clean towel laid out and, should he need it, a new toothbrush in its plastic case. He thought he might manage a few more pages of *The Man Who Liked Slow Tomatoes* before dropping off, but when he woke in the morning, the book had fallen to the floor, unread.

***

Wherever he'd gone in those two hours, Anderson had come back with a bottle of Vodka. Stolichnaya. Perhaps he'd had it with him all along. He sat there, close to the entrance to the tent, drinking steadily. Rebecca tried to get the children to eat something but to little avail. She forced herself to try some of the corned beef, though it was something she'd never liked. The children drank water, nibbled biscuits. and moped.

The rain outside increased until it began seeping under one corner of the tent.

Billie lay down, sucking her thumb, and, for once, Rebecca made no attempt to stop her. If Keiron, huddled into a blanket near her feet, was asleep or not she wasn't sure.

The bottle was now half empty.

Anderson stared straight ahead, seeing something she couldn't see.

'Terry?'

At the softness of her voice, he flinched.

'How long is it since you got any sleep?'

Whenever she had awoken in the early hours after they'd arrived, he had been sitting, shoulders hunched, alert and keeping guard.

'How long?'

'I don't know. A long time.'

'What's wrong?'

For an answer he lifted the bottle to his lips.

'Perhaps you should talk to someone? About what's troubling you? Perhaps...'

'Stop it! Just fucking stop it! Shut up!'

'Stop what?'

'Wheedling fucking round me.' He mimicked her voice. 'Perhaps you should talk to someone, Terry? As if you gave a shit.'

'I do.'

'Yeah?' He laughed. 'You don't give a shit about me and I don't give a shit about you. Not any more.'

'Then why are we here?'

'Because of them. Because they have to know.'

'Know what?'

He moved suddenly. 'Wake them. Go on, wake them up.'

'No, look, they're exhausted. Let them sleep.'

But Billie was already stirring and Keiron was awake.

Anderson took another long swallow from the bottle. His skin was sallow and beads of perspiration stood out on his forehead and his temples. When he started talking, his voice seemed distant, even in the confines of the tent.

'We were on patrol, just routine. There'd been a firefight a couple of days before, so we were more on our guard than usual. Against snipers but also for explosives. IEDs. We were passing this house and this woman came out, just her face showing, part of her face, the eyes,

and she's waving her arms and wailing and
pointing back towards the house as if there's
something wrong, and Sean, he jumps down,
even though we're telling him not to be stupid,
and the next thing we know, he's followed her
to the doorway, and the next after that he's
been shot. One gets him in the body and knocks
him back, but he's wearing his chest plate,
thank Christ, so that's all right, but the next
one takes him in the neck. By now we're returning fire and the woman's disappeared, nowhere
to be fucking seen, Sean's leaking blood into the
fucking ground, so we drag him out of there,
back into the vehicle and head back to camp.'

Beside Rebecca, Keiron, wide-eyed, listened
enthralled. Billie clutched her mother's hand
and flinched each time her father swore.

'He died, that's the thing. Sean. The bullet'd
torn an artery and the bleeding wouldn't stop.
By the time we reached camp, he was dead. He
was our mate, a laugh. A real laugh. Always saw
the funny side. Just a young bloke. Twenty-one.
And stupid. Young and stupid. He'd wanted to
help.' Anderson took a quick swallow and wiped

his mouth. 'Two days later, we went back. Went back at night, five of us. We'd been drinking beforehand, pretty heavily, talking about what had happened, what they'd done to Sean.'

Rebecca shivered and hugged the children close.

'We went in under cover of darkness. There was no moon, I remember, not then. Sometimes it'd be, you know, huge, filling half the fucking sky, but that night there was nothing. Just a few stars. Everyone inside was sleeping. Women. Men.' He paused. 'Children. Soon as we got inside one of the men reached for his gun, he'd been sleeping with it, under the blankets, and that's when we started firing. Firing at anything that moved. One of the women, she came running at us, screaming, and Steve, he says, 'That's her. That's her, the lyin' bitch,' and, of course, dressed like she was, like they all were, he had no way of knowing, but that didn't stop him all but emptying his magazine into her.'

'That's enough,' Rebecca said. 'Enough.'

'There was a girl,' Anderson said, ignoring

her, 'hiding in one of the other rooms. Twelve, maybe thirteen. I don't know. Could've been younger. Steve grabbed hold of her and threw her down on the floor and then one of the others started to tear off her clothes.'

'Stop,' Rebecca said. 'Please stop. They don't need to hear this.'

'Yes, they do! Yes, they do!'

Keiron was not looking, refusing to look, pressing his face into his mother's side.

'We all knew what was going to happen. Steve's standing over her, pulling off the last of her things, and she calls him a name and spits at him and he leans down and punches her in the face, and then he's on his knees, unzipping himself, and we're all watching, a couple cheering him on, give it to her, give it to her, clapping like it's some game, and that's when I tell him, I tell him twice to stop and he just carries on and I couldn't, I couldn't, I couldn't just stand there and watch — she was just a child! — and I shot him, through the back of the head. Blood and gunk all over the girl's face and she wriggles out from under and grabs her clothes and runs and we're left standing there. All except for Steve. He was my mate, too, they all were, and I'd killed him over some girl who, even before that happened, would've happily seen us blown to smithereens.'

He wiped away some of the sweat that was running into his eyes. Tears were running soundlessly down Rebecca's face.

'We all agreed, the rest of us, to claim he'd got caught in the crossfire. After what had happened, no one was going to want to tell the truth.'

'Except you,' Rebecca said.

'This is different.' He nodded towards the children. 'They needed to know.'

'Why?'

'So they can understand.'

And his hands reached down towards his rifle.

Not long after first light, a police helicopter, flying low over the forest, reported a woman and two children standing in a small clearing, waving a makeshift flag.

Armed officers secured the area. Rebecca and the children were escorted to the perimeter, where paramedics were waiting. Anderson was found lying inside the tent, a dark cagoule covering his face, his discharged weapon close at hand. At the hospital later, after she had rested and the medical staff had examined her, Rebecca slowly began to tell Resnick and a female liaison officer her story. The children were in another room with a nurse and their maternal grandmother.

Later still, relishing the chance to stretch his legs, Resnick walked with Kiley the short distance through the city centre to the railway station. Already, a rush edition of the *Post* was on the streets. It would be national news for a moment, a day, page one beneath the fold, then a short column on page six, a paragraph on page thirteen. Forgotten. One of those things that happen, stress of combat, balance of mind disturbed. Rebecca had told the police her husband's story, as well as she remembered, what he had seen, the attack at night, the confusion, the young Iraqi girl, the fellow soldier caught in the crossfire and killed in front of his eyes. He hadn't been able to sleep, she said, not since that happened. I don't think he could face going back to it again.

'Not what you wanted, Jack,' Resnick said, shaking his hand.

The 15.30 to London St. Pancras was on time.

'None of us,' Kiley said.

'We'll catch that game some time.'

'Yes. I'd like that.'

Kiley hurried down the steps on to the platform.

He phoned Jennie Calder from the train. In a little over two hours time he would be crossing towards the flats where Mary Anderson lived and climbing the stairs, welcome on the mat, but not for him, her face when she opened the door ajar with tears.

Any Notts County supporters reading this will forgive me, I trust, for playing fast and loose with the details of the club's highly successful F.A. Cup run in 1990/91. Manchester City not Charlton Athletic. Come on, you Pies!